Ginet

S0-AWZ-526

Arthur's Dad

Illustrations
by Anne Villeneuve

Translated
by Sarah Cummins

Formac Publishing Company Limited
Halifax, Nova Scotia
1991

Originally published as Le père d'Arthur

Copyright © 1989 la courte échelle

Translation copyright © 1991 by Formac Publishing Limited.

Canadian Cataloguing in Publication Data
Anfousse, Ginette, 1944-

   [Père d'Arthur. English]

   Arthur's dad

   (First novel series)

   For children aged 7-10.

   Translation of Le père d'Arthur.

   ISBN 0-88780-094-7 (pbk.) ISBN 0-88780-095-5 (bound)

i. Villeneuve, Anne. II Title. III. Title: Père d'Arthur. English. IV. Series.
PS8551.N42P4713 1991 jC843'.54 C91-097684-8
PZ7.A53Ar 1991

Formac Publishing Company Limited
5502 Atlantic Street
Halifax, N.S. B3H 1G4

Printed and bound in Canada

Table of contents

1
Babysitters, bowling and bassets

Mr. Goodberry was not in a very good mood that morning. He was already on his sixth cup of coffee, and he hadn't yet spoken a word to his son.

Arthur, seated beside him at the breakfast table, silently spread strawberry jam on his fourth piece of toast.

When his dad was in one of these moods, he knew it was best to keep quiet, lie low, and wait.

"Should I put banana slices on top of the jam?" Arthur wondered. He reached out for a banana, his favourite fruit.

His father made a strange groaning sound, so Arthur decided to forget about the banana for now. He bit into his toast.

Mr. Goodberry took his head in his hands and sighed. "It's enough to make me tear my hair out. To tear my hair right out!"

Arthur raised his eyes to his father's face.

"You can't, Dad. You don't have any hair left."

This was, indeed, the truth. Arthur's father had a magnificent mustache, but the top of his head had no more hair than the electric kettle, which at that moment began to whistle again.

William Goodberry shuffled over to the counter and unplugged the kettle. For the seventh time that morning he filled his cup with boiling water. Then he burst out, "She was the last one on my list, Arthur. THE VERY LAST ONE! And now, like the other twenty-two babysitters before her, she will NEVER come here again!"

Arthur could believe it. Valerie Almond would definitely never babysit for him again. Arthur's face brightened and he rewarded his father with the sweetest, most triumphant of smiles.

Despite his promise never again to do such a thing, Arthur had locked Valerie Almond in the closet twice last week. He couldn't help himself. Arthur just couldn't stand having a babysitter.

Right now, he felt like going to play in the park with his friends, but as his father was still gazing at him morosely, he didn't dare ask.

To sweeten his dad's mood, Arthur reached out for the sugar bowl. Clumsily he knocked over the box of cereal and the milk carton.

The next instant, milk was spreading across the table, streaming toward his father, splashing onto his striped pyjamas, and dripping down his legs.

"I didn't do it on purpose, Dad!" Arthur cried hastily. "I was only going to put sugar in your coffee for you."

"YEEOW YEEOW YEEOW," Mr. Goodberry squealed. He held his legs apart as the milk seeped into his slippers.

The look on his face reminded Arthur of a sad basset hound. Arthur knew all about basset hounds. He had a super collec-

tion of stuffed basset hounds in his room.

To keep his father from roaring like a dragon, Arthur bounded over to the sink, grabbed a rag, and got down on all fours to wipe up the mess.

Then, he pulled off his father's slippers and wiped his toes dry, one by one. A good thing, too, as Mr. Goodberry was slowly turning red with rage.

Just to be sure his father truly forgave him, Arthur planted a big, sloppy kiss on top of his egg-like head, right where the skin was as smooth and soft as a baby's.

William Goodberry's teeth gradually unclenched. Despondently he said, "My bowling match is on Tuesday, Arthur. Do you have a solution?"

Arthur raised his head. Grinning broadly, he replied, "Yeah, I've got a solution! Either you quit bowling...or you take me with you."

Mr. Goodberry's face drooped like a basset hound again. In a single gulp he swallowed his seventh cup of coffee of the day.

2
The Bowldozer

A little later, Arthur was calmly getting dressed in his room. He was tidily stowing his pyjamas under his pillow when he heard a blood-curdling shriek, followed by, "ARTHUR! Come here at once!"

"Hmm," thought Arthur. "Either my father has got his foot stuck in the spokes of my bike, or else he has walked through a puddle of my glue."

Wrong. And wrong again.

When Arthur came down, Mr. Goodberry was standing over the telephone receiver that had fallen onto the living room floor. He was muttering over and over, "They hung up on me! They hung up on me!"

He pointed an accusing finger at his son. "Do you know, Arthur, who dared to do such a thing to your father?"

Without stopping to think, Arthur answered, "Was it Al Doloroso, who works in the shop with you? Or was it Charlotte Peever, who drags you bowling while I have to stay with a babysitter?"

"No, it wasn't, Arthur." His father was annoyed. "It wasn't either one of them. It was the Babysitters' Association of

Hinksville. They know all."

Puzzled, Arthur looked at his shoes. Then he lifted his eyes to his father.

"Do they even know about the baking soda in Miss Jostman's tea?"

"Yes," answered his father. "They even know about the baking soda in Miss Jostman's tea."

In a woeful voice he went on, "They also know about Hugo Wisenheimer and the lasso tricks. And about Rosaleen Wong and the fake tarantulas. And about your itching powder. Your stink bombs. They even know about poor Carol Trimble."

Arthur looked down again. He recalled very clearly a certain

evening when his father had grown angrier than he ever had before. That was the time Arthur had locked himself in his room and started screaming his head off.

The poor babysitter had completely flipped out. Arthur's father had returned home to find ten neighbours, two policemen, and three firemen in the house.

Arthur never tried that one again.

Now Mr. Goodberry was pacing back and forth in the living room, scratching his head, and muttering sorrowfully, "They say you're a MONSTER, Arthur. You are such a notorious monster that absolutely no one will ever, ever agree to babysit you."

Arthur began to scratch his own head, too. Then he said, "What's wrong with being a MONSTER? Your store is full of monsters."

Mr. Goodberry nodded his head. "Just what Charlotte Peever said. She said it was the store that gave you all these ideas. She suggested I sell the store."

Arthur's eyes stung with tears. He was so proud of his father's tricks and jokes store.

His friends all agreed with him that Creepy Crawlies was more fun than any other store in Hinksville.

Arthur ran to his room, calling behind him, "That's not a good idea, Dad!"

And since in his house everyone always said everything twice, he called out again, "Not a very good idea at all!"

Ten minutes later, Arthur was lining his stuffed basset hounds up in a neat row on his comforter. He was lying on his stomach daydreaming, when he heard a blood-curdling shriek.

Then, "ARTHUR! Come here at once!"

"Hmm," Arthur thought. "Either my father has stuck his nose in his tobacco pouch, which I have filled with itching powder. Or else my tractor collection has fallen on his head."

Wrong. And wrong again.

Someone else had dared to hang up on Mr. Goodberry. This time it was Charlotte Peever, the Bowldozer.

****

The next day Arthur went to his father's store. Mr. Goodberry had just received a large shipment of water pistols.

Arthur tried them all out. First he aimed at Al Doloroso's old cap, then he aimed at his father's freshly-polished shoes.

It didn't take long to figure out which water pistol shot the biggest stream of water and which had the most accurate aim. At about five-thirty, things started to go wrong. But it wasn't Arthur's fault.

How was he supposed to know that a customer would come in the store at just the instant he was aiming at the bell over the door? SPLASH! Right in the middle of the customer's forehead.

Fortunately, it was a regular customer who was just stopping by to pick up his weekly supply of firecrackers. The poor guy stood there smiling foolishly.

Mr. Goodberry did not think it was funny at all. The top of his

bald head turned red as a beet again.

Before things got any worse, Arthur quickly began to put away the water pistols. He could see that his dad was not feeling in tip-top form.

Al Doloroso whispered in his ear, "Your father's acting much too solemn to sell stink bombs or itching powder today. All day long he's been muttering 'I can't leave a seven-year-old child alone at home. It's not easy being a single parent. If only Charlotte understood.'"

It was obvious to Arthur that Charlotte Peever would never understand.

3
Babas and baby chicks

On Tuesday, as it happened, Arthur spent a super-fantastic evening with his father. He even let his dad win at dominos, and then Crazy Eights, and then Monopoly.

Arthur wanted to make his father happy, and for a while it worked. The proof was that on Tuesday, Wednesday, Thursday, and Friday, his father did not mention bowling or babysitters or Charlotte Peever.

Arthur was so happy he could have jumped for joy. Unfortunately, on Saturday the bubble burst.

Arthur was busy at the store helping his father by putting labels on boxes of false noses when the telephone rang. He rushed to answer. It was the person he hated most in the whole world.

He yelled at the top of his lungs, "Dad! It's the Bowldozer! Should I tell her you never want to see her again? Or should I just hang up on her?"

Furious, Mr. Goodberry grabbed the receiver and stammered, "Is that you, Charlotte?"

Arthur no longer felt like jumping for joy. He felt like barricading himself in the closet and

screaming his head off.

"Guess what, Arthur!" His father twirled around in front of him. "Charlotte isn't angry any more. She has invited both of us to her house for dinner tomorrow."

Arthur turned without a word and went to the back of the store to stock up on creepy crawlies.

****

Before leaving for Charlotte Peever's house, Mr. Goodberry searched through all of Arthur's pockets. He only frowned a bit when he discovered the three latex frogs and a bat that Arthur had concealed.

Arthur pretended to sulk, then turned his head so his father wouldn't see him snicker.

His father had neglected to frisk his running shoes this time. The rubber snake was still in Arthur's sock where he had hidden it.

At the dinner table, the Bowldozer had Mr. Goodberry sit across from her, while Arthur was placed all by himself at one end.

This did not keep Arthur from staring at the enormous wart that Charlotte had on her chin, or the hair growing from it, as long as a cat's whisker.

Arthur was now absolutely certain that Charlotte Peever hated children. Why else would she serve such disgusting pumpkin soup? And this funny little bird surrounded by baby carrots and baby turnips? Even baby onions!

Arthur pushed his plate away. "I don't eat baby chicks," he announced.

Pursing her lips, the witch replied, "These are quail, Arthur, not baby chicks."

Arthur didn't care. Abandoning his plate, he watched Charlotte Peever swallow her baby onions whole. Disgusted, he lost all desire to eat.

At dessert time, Charlotte brought in a silver tray. Mr. Goodberry said quickly, "Arthur, these aren't babies; they're babas. Rum babas."

Arthur had never eaten a rum baba before, but he knew, with Charlotte Peever, that he had better be careful. He stuck his finger into the baba. Yuck!

He was right to be worried. It tasted like lighter fluid. Arthur made an awful face.

Then the Bowldozer started to wriggle around on her chair. She scrunched up her nose. The hair in her wart stood on end. She bared her teeth. Then she said breathily, "William, I have some good news for you!"

Arthur immediately became suspicious. He stuck his finger in the baba again.

The Doozer went on: "I've found a new BABYSITTER for Arthur. And what a treasure! She's very good with children who are...well, who are...well, you know what I mean."

Arthur's father, like a coward, lowered his eyes.

Arthur got up from the table and said bitterly, "Excuse me, I have to go to the bathroom."

Once in the bathroom, he took

off his shoe. As he pulled the snake out, it wriggled just like a real one. Arthur was pleased.

He opened a little door underneath the sink. Bleach and detergent were stored there. Above the sink, he saw cosmetics and perfume.

Arthur was so upset he felt like pouring bleach in the cologne bottle and detergent in the make-up. Dangling his snake, he look around and spotted the bottle of mouthwash. He slipped the snake into the apple-green liquid.

Satisfied with his work, Arthur put his shoe back on and returned to the dinner table to poke his baba around some more.

He spent the rest of the evening stretched out on the living room carpet, resentfully watching the witch and his father as they discussed five-pin and ten-pin, strikes, and gutterballs, while listening to the opera.

It was so boring that Arthur fell asleep. Later, Mr. Goodberry took him home without waking him.

****

The next morning, Arthur was lying on his bed surrounded by his twelve basset hounds when he heard a blood-curdling shriek followed by, "ARTHUR! Come here at once!"

His father was on the phone when Arthur walked into his room. He was murmuring into the receiver, "Calm down, my dear, please calm down!"

From the distressed look on his father's face, Arthur knew that the Bowldozer had just used her mouthwash.

4
Ambidextrous Annie

When the new babysitter rang the doorbell on Tuesday, Arthur was ready. He was hiding inside a big cardboard box. This was part of the great plan he had devised to get rid of the twenty-third babysitter.

Arthur had cut out a door on one side of the box and on the door he had written DO NOT ENTER. He had closed the door carefully, then cut a tiny opening that he could see through without anyone seeing him.

Through the hole, Arthur was now watching a pair of high-heeled shoes tripping over the kitchen tiles.

He was astonished to hear a KNOCK KNOCK KNOCK on

his box, and then a horrible BANG, an obnoxious voice saying, "I bet Arthur is in here, Mum!"

Arthur didn't even have time to wonder what was going on before his shelter began to sway and shake. Then he heard another awful BANG and the obnoxious voice saying, "Arthur, I'm warning you! I know all about you. And I just want to let you know that I am AMBIDEXTROUS!"

Arthur had no idea what AMBIDEXTROUS meant. But he was sure beyond all doubt that his great plan had crumbled into a thousand tiny pieces.

He bit his lip, thinking resentfully of his father who had once again abandoned him.

He peeked through the hole again and was stupefied to see two red braids, a million freckles, and a horrible mouth with its tongue impudently sticking out at him.

"You flyswatter," Arthur muttered under his breath.

Just before an ear-splitting BING BA DI BANG! rained down on the roof, Arthur heard the voice say, "I'm eight years old. And watch out, I BITE!"

"I'm not surprised," Arthur shot back. "Girls either scratch, or they bite."

He heard a horrid cackle, like the laughter of a fiend. The voice said, "My name is Annie. And if you don't come out of there, I'm going to go up and look around your room."

Arthur was furious. Clenching his fists he yelled at the top of his lungs at the horrible red-headed fiend, "If you dare to set foot in my room, I'll...I'll..."

He stopped short. He had suddenly remembered that the fiend was ambidextrous. Since he was not sure what sort of power she possessed, he didn't dare threaten her.

He thought it would be best to come out of his hiding place. He pushed on the door. Nothing happened. The ambidextrous fiend had blocked it with a chair.

Beside himself with rage, Arthur took a flying leap at the door. But now, the fiend had removed the chair. Arthur tumbled out in a sorry heap at the feet of Mrs. McCubbin, his new baby-sitter who was Annie's mother. He scrambled to his feet and ran to his room.

Too late. Annie was already there. She was brazenly sitting on his bed, rocking the smallest of his basset hounds in her arms, and crooning to it: "You're just like Freddy, my real baby basset."

Arthur thought angrily to himself, "Should I poke out both her eyes, or should I scalp off both her braids?"

Instead he dumped his entire collection of creepy crawlies over her head. But Annie didn't scream. Far worse: she seemed to love it.

"You lucky dog, you've got millions!" she said.

Arthur was humiliated. He decided to change tactics. He would sweeten her up. He would impress her.

Arthur showed Annie everything he had in his secret drawers. Then they spent nearly two hours in his room squirting and frightening each other, sneezing, and laughing until the tears ran down their cheeks.

Later, they both crawled into the cardboard box and munched on chocolate-chip cookies Mrs. McCubbin had baked.

Safe from any eavesdroppers, Arthur told Annie all about Charlotte Peever. He told her about the repulsive hair growing out of the wart, the pumpkin soup and the baby chicks, and especially the endless bowling matches to which she was always dragging his dad.

At exactly nine o'clock that night, Arthur whispered to Annie, "I would really like to get rid of Charlotte Peever, FOR GOOD."

At exactly 9:01, Annie whispered back, "Don't worry. I know all about her, and I have a

recipe. Before the week is up, your father will feel that he never wants to see her again.

"You'll have to steal several hairs from your father's mustache," she went on. "I'll take care of the hair growing from Charlotte Peever's wart."

Mr. Goodberry got quite a surprise when he walked in the door that evening. No screams! No policemen! No babysitters tied to a post!

Arthur and Annie had fallen asleep in the cardboard box. Mrs. McCubbin was reading a book about Dracula and his fatal bites.

Mr. Goodberry was so thrilled that he made a big cup of tea for Mrs. McCubbin. Then together, they finished all the chocolate-chip cookies.

5
Arthur's father's mustache

The next week was the longest week Arthur had ever spent in his entire life. He couldn't wait until Saturday, especially since he had found out what AM-BIDEXTROUS meant.

Arthur had asked his father. Mr. Goodberry had replied absent-mindedly, "It means someone who can do anything with either the right hand or the left hand."

"Anything?" Arthur had

wanted to make sure.

"Anything," his father had repeated firmly.

Arthur was impressed. He no longer had the slightest doubts about the infinite powers of his new friend.

Arthur had cut off half of his father's mustache, just as Annie had said. It was easy. He just waited until his father started to snore, then CLICK CLACK with the scissors, that was all.

Of course, Arthur was punished. How was he supposed to know that his bald-headed father set so much store by his mustache?

****

It was nearly seven o'clock on

Saturday evening. Arthur was pacing the floor. At seven on the dot, Annie arrived. She and Arthur ran upstairs to his room and shut the door.

Annie reached into her pocket and took out a small folded handkerchief. She unfolded it to reveal a long hair like a cat's whisker.

Arthur's heart began to beat faster. He gave Annie the little package he had prepared. She smiled.

Fascinated and excited, Arthur watched as she ground up Charlotte Peever's whisker with the hairs from his father's mustache.

She added a pinch of cayenne pepper, a bit of hot mustard, two hamster droppings, and a wee dram of Seven-Up.

First she mixed it all together with her right hand. Then she mixed it all together with her left hand.

She chanted a magic spell as she worked. Then she poured the potion into two small bottles and whispered into Arthur's ear, "For next Tuesday!"

"Great!" Arthur whispered back. "That's the day of the bowling tournament."

"Perfect!" whispered Annie. "On Tuesday, you have to pour all of this bottle into your father's coffee. I will pour the other bottle into Charlotte Peever's herbal tea."

Annie and Arthur were so excited that Mrs. McCubbin had to bake them a whole mountain of molasses cookies to get them to settle down.

As they all knew how fond Arthur's father was of cookies, they left a plateful especially for him.

6
The big day

Finally the big day arrived. At the very instant that Arthur's father was choking on his coffee, Charlotte Peever was just making herself a cup of herbal tea.

As usual, she drained the cup in a single gulp. She tried to spit the tea out again, but it was already burning down her gullet.

She wailed like a lost soul and

whimpered weakly. It had been such a difficult week for her!

She had never discovered who had pulled the hair out of her wart, or how it had been done, and now she had proof that someone was trying to poison her! Trying to poison her on the very day of her bowling tournament! The poisoner was probably trying to rattle her, to keep her from winning.

Charlotte Peever's mood was extremely foul when she finally arrived at the bowling tournament. She looked high and low for Mr. Goodberry, her partner, and screamed at everyone like a harpy.

****

Mrs. McCubbin was baking almond cookies for Mr. Goodberry. Almond cookies were his favourite kind. Arthur and Annie were hiding in the cardboard box, spying on Mr. Goodberry through the peep-hole.

They were distressed to see him still wandering through the kitchen, sticking his fingers in the cookie dough and filching almonds.

Finally, he checked his watch and cried out, "I'm already half an hour late! Charlotte will never forgive me!"

With great relief, Arthur watched his father go out the door.

"It's about time," he whispered to Annie. "Now all we can do is wait until he comes back. We mustn't fall asleep."

Arthur and Annie had a very long wait. They played Crazy Eights. Annie won, and then she sighed, "You know, afterwards, you and me...it will be all over."

Arthur, bewildered, just stared at her.

"You know," explained Annie. "No more Bowldozer, no more babysitter. No more babysitter, no more Annie!"

Arthur felt like crying. But Annie said, "Don't start snivelling like a baby. Ambidextrous people can always come up with a solution."

Then once again, Arthur watched as Annie began to mix up a strange potion. She used a hair from her mother's head, what was left of Arthur's father's mustache, some plush from a stuffed basset hound, and a bit of milk.

Fascinated, Arthur watched as she stirred first with her right hand, then with her left hand. She muttered a magic spell as she worked.

She called it a "love potion," and had just finished when Mr. Goodberry came in the door, whistling. He was much earlier than expected.

He didn't appear in the least upset. He was even chuckling as he plugged in the kettle to make tea.

Arthur was worried. "Either my father has just won the bowling tournament, or the mustard potion has failed to take effect."

Wrong. And wrong again.

The mustard potion had indeed taken effect, and Mr. Goodberry had lost the bowling tournament.

Charlotte Peever, black with rage, had stomped out of the bowling alley after throwing all her balls in the gutter.

While Mr. Goodberry was telling Mrs. McCubbin all about Charlotte Peever's antics, Arthur and Annie stole into the kitchen. They emptied the bottle of love potion into the teapot.

Grinning from ear to ear, they watched Mr. Goodberry and Mrs. McCubbin drain the teapot down to the last drop.

They were certain that the love potion had already taken effect. How could they be so sure? Well, their parents did not gag as they drank the tea down, gazing deep into each other's eyes.

Arthur and Annie knew that they'd be seeing a lot of each other in future.

The First Novel series

Award-winning books for young readers — look for these and other titles in the series!

That's Enough, Maddie
by Louise LeBlanc

Maddie has quite a problem. Her whole family, her dad, her mom, and the baby are getting on her nerves.

What to do? Maddie decides she'll run away from home...but what do you do when it's six o'clock and it's time for supper?

The Swank Prank
by Bertrand Gauthier

Hank and Frank Swank are twins. They look exactly alike, but they are not alike in any other way! Trying to be the smartest kids in school takes a lot of hard work and they have to learn to get along. Will they be able to do it?

Mooch and Me
by Gilles Gauthier

Carl and his best friend, Mooch, are nine. But, Mooch is a dog and that makes him sixty three! He is old, deaf, mostly blind, and gets Carl into loads of trouble. But Carl thinks he is the best dog that ever lived!